STAR WARS
FORCES OF DESTINY™
AHSOKA & PADMÉ

Writer
Beth Revis

Artist & Colorist
Valentina Pinto

Letterer
Tom B. Long

Assistant Editor
Peter Adrian Behravesh

Editors
Bobby Curnow & Denton J. Tipton

ABDOBOOKS.COM

Reinforced library bound edition published in 2019 by Spotlight, a division of ABDO, PO Box 398166, Minneapolis, Minnesota 55439. Spotlight produces high-quality reinforced library bound editions for schools and libraries.
Published by agreement with IDW.

Printed in the United States of America, North Mankato, Minnesota.
092018
012019

Library of Congress Control Number: 2018945158

Publisher's Cataloging-in-Publication Data

Names: Revis, Beth, author. | Pinto, Valentina, illustrator.
Title: Ahsoka & Padmé / by Beth Revis; illustrated by Valentina Pinto.
Description: Minneapolis, MN : Spotlight, 2019 | Series: Star wars: Forces of destiny
Summary: Ahsoka and Padmé prepare for a controversial dinner party, but when they notice someone has set the table incorrectly, they discover a disguised assassin.
Identifiers: ISBN 9781532142925 (lib. bdg.)
Subjects: LCSH: Star Wars fiction--Juvenile fiction. | Space warfare--Juvenile fiction. | Women heroes--Juvenile fiction. | Extraterrestrial beings--Juvenile fiction. | Good and evil--Juvenile fiction.
Classification: DDC 741.5--dc23

Spotlight

A Division of ABDO
abdobooks.com

KZZZCH

THUMP

I YIELD.

GOOD MATCH, BARRISS.
NOT REALLY, AHSOKA.

WHY WOULD YOU SAY THAT?
HAD THIS BEEN A TRUE BATTLE, YOU NEVER WOULD HAVE THROWN YOUR LIGHT-SABER AT YOUR ENEMY.
YEAH, BUT IT WORKED THIS TIME. I KNEW WHAT YOU'D DO.
TRAINING SESSIONS ARE ABOUT PREPARING US FOR THE REAL WORLD AND THE REAL BATTLES WE MUST FACE. NOT JUST TO WIN BY WHATEVER MEANS.
I SAW AN OPPORTUNITY, AND I TOOK IT.

SHOULD YOU HAVE?
WHAT DO YOU MEAN?
YOU LEARNED NOTHING IN THIS SESSION, EVEN IF YOU WON. THIS WILL NOT HELP YOU IN THE FUTURE.

MASTER ANAKIN WOULD SAY IT DOESN'T MATTER HOW YOU WIN AS LONG AS YOU DO.

OUR MASTERS HAVE VERY DIFFERENT TRAINING STYLES. MASTER LUMINARA TEACHES ME THAT THE FORMS REQUIRE PATIENCE.
YOU WERE SO EAGER TO WIN THAT YOU FORGOT THE FORMS.
I HAVE PATIENCE!
FORMS DON'T HELP IN A REAL BATTLE.
OR AT LEAST THEY DON'T HELP ME.

LET ME SEE YOUR LIGHTSABERS.
YOU OFTEN USE A VARIANT OF FORM FIVE, BUT IF YOU'D USED FORM SIX AGAINST ME, IT WOULD HAVE BEEN MORE EFFECTIVE.
HEY, SOMETIMES IMPROVISING WORKS JUST AS WELL.
AS EVIDENCED BY TODAY'S MATCH.

OUR MASTERS JUST HAVE VERY DIFFERENT WAYS OF TRAINING US, I SUPPOSE.
THAT IS SOMETHING WE CAN DEFINITELY AGREE ON!
NO ONE'S LIKE MASTER ANAKIN.
THANKS FOR THE MATCH TODAY.
I LEARNED A LOT.
I HOPE YOU DID AS WELL.
MAYBE MEDITATING WILL HELP CLEAR MY MIND.

MASTER ANAKIN HAS TRAINED ME WELL...
...BUT BARRISS IS RIGHT. THAT WASN'T A GOOD WIN.

I HAVE TO THINK LIKE A JEDI.
I'M STILL NOT GOOD ENOUGH.
KNOCK KNOCK
YES? PLEASE COME IN.

AHSOKA, I CAME—
OH! I'M SORRY. I DIDN'T KNOW YOU WERE MEDITATING.
I AM FINISHED NOW. IT'S SO GOOD TO SEE YOU, SENATOR AMIDALA.

BUT I'M SURPRISED YOU'VE COME HERE TO THE TEMPLE.
IS EVERYTHING ALL RIGHT?

NO, I'M AFRAID IT ISN'T.
TOMORROW, I'M GIVING A DINNER PARTY FOR THE ARTHURIAN DELEGATES.

IT'S A VERY IMPORTANT MEETING. COULD YOU COME AND KEEP AN EYE OUT?
BUT SHOULDN'T YOU GET SOMEONE—
—BETTER—
—MORE QUALIFIED?

ANAKIN IS AWAY ON A MISSION. I TRUST YOU.
JUST A QUICK CHECK OF MY BUILDING BEFOREHAND. I KNOW IT'S A BIG FAVOR.
BUT YOU HAVE CAPTAIN TYPHO. SURELY HE CAN SECURE THE PREMISES. AND YOUR HANDMAIDENS WILL PROTECT YOU.

I TRUST *YOU.*

"TRAINING SESSIONS ARE ABOUT PREPARING US FOR THE REAL WORLD AND THE REAL BATTLES WE MUST FACE."

OKAY. I'LL DO IT.
THANK YOU.
THIS EVENT IS VERY IMPORTANT. NOTHING CAN GO WRONG.

"TYPHO WILL BE THERE. BUT DORMÉ HAD TO RETURN TO NABOO FOR A FAMILY MATTER. I HAVE OTHER HANDMAIDENS, OF COURSE, BUT..."

...I NEED A JEDI. I NEED YOU.

OF COURSE.

THE NEXT DAY.
THANK YOU ALL FOR BEING HERE. AS YOU KNOW, TODAY'S MEETING IS INCREDIBLY IMPORTANT, AND WITH DORMÉ NOT HERE TO OVERSEE THINGS FOR ME, I WANTED TO TOUCH BASE AND STRESS JUST HOW VITAL A ROLE YOU WILL EACH PLAY.
"ARTHURIANS ARE HIGHLY CONCERNED WITH PROPER ETIQUETTE. THEY ARE CONSIDERING JOINING THE REPUBLIC BECAUSE THEY FEEL THE SEPARATISTS ARE RUDE AND DISRESPECTFUL TO ARTHURIA. THEIR POTENTIAL ALLIANCE IS CRUCIAL.
"FORMAL DRESS IS REQUIRED AT ALL TIMES IN THE ARTHURIAN DELEGATES' PRESENCE.
"WHITE IS A COLOR OF RESPECT, WORN ONLY BY AUTHORITIES.
"ARTHURIANS HAVE TASTE BUDS IN THEIR HANDS, AND ONLY TAKE THEIR GLOVES OFF IN PUBLIC TO EAT. UTENSILS ARE INSULTING.
"EYE CONTACT SHOULD ONLY BE MADE WHILE SPEAKING, OTHERWISE DIVERT YOUR GAZE."

YOUR JOB IS TO ENSURE THAT THE ARTHURIANS FEEL RESPECTED AND AT EASE HERE.
WEAR YOUR FORMAL ROBES, DON'T MAKE EYE CONTACT, AND SET THE TABLE WITHOUT UTENSILS.

I'M RELYING ON YOU ALL. ARE MY INSTRUCTIONS CLEAR?
YES, MA'AM.
YES.
YES, SENATOR.
YOU CAN COUNT ON US.
YES.
WHAT ABOUT SECURITY?

WE WILL HAVE THE FULL SUPPORT OF THE ROYAL NABOO SECURITY FORCES ON HAND.
CAPTAIN TYPHO WILL GO OVER ADDITIONAL PROCEDURES WITH YOU ALL.
"I HAVE LITTLE DOUBT THAT WE WILL BE WELL PROTECTED."

RIGHT, LET'S RUN THE DRILL ONCE MORE. WE *WILL* ENSURE THE DELEGATES ARRIVE SAFELY FOR THEIR MEETING WITH SENATOR AMIDALA!

YOU HEARD THE SENATOR! ALL FOOD PASSES INSPECTION BEFORE IT LEAVES THIS KITCHEN.
AND NO ELBINA PEPPER! IT MAKES THE ARTHURIANS' HANDS ITCH.

PADMÉ?
IT SEEMS AS IF YOU THOUGHT OF EVERYTHING.

I JUST FINISHED SECURING THE PERIMETER OF THE BUILDING. THE OUTSIDE IS CLEAR.
I APPRECIATE YOU HELPING OUT, AHSOKA.
THESE NEGOTIATIONS WITH THE ARTHURIAN DELEGATES ARE CRITICAL, AND THERE ARE A LOT OF PEOPLE WHO DON'T WANT THEM TO HAPPEN.
YOU KNOW, IT MIGHT NOT BE SUCH A BAD IDEA IF YOU STICK AROUND.
THANK YOU, SENATOR AMIDALA.
BUT IT'S NOT REALLY MY PLACE TO MINGLE WITH POLITICIANS.

I DO HAVE ONE QUESTION, THOUGH, IF YOU DON'T MIND.
OF COURSE, AHSOKA.

WHY DID YOU SET THE TABLE WITH UTENSILS? THE ARTHURIAN DELEGATES NEVER USE THEM AND MIGHT FIND IT INSULTING.

I WAS VERY SPECIFIC IN MY INSTRUCTIONS.
EXCUSE ME?
SHE LOOKS LIKE KARTÉ, BUT THERE'S SOMETHING DIFFERENT ABOUT HER...

WHAT IS THE MEANING OF THIS?

PEW
TNSK

CRASH

IS SHE ON THE GUEST LIST?
UH, NO.

PEW PEW

TAZING

UH!

ZOT

CLICK
BEEP
BEEP
BEEP

AHSOKA, THERE'S A BOMB!
SEND IT TO ME!

THUD

VMMMMMM

FWOOM

BOOM

CRASH

YOU KNOW, YOU REMIND ME A LOT OF ANAKIN SOMETIMES.
THANKS.
WELL, IT LOOKS LIKE THESE NEGOTIATIONS WILL HAVE TO BE POSTPONED.

IN THAT CASE, I GUESS I WILL STAY. I'D HATE TO SEE ALL THAT FOOD GO TO WASTE.

YOU FOUND KARTÉ?
WE WERE LOOKING FOR HER DURING THE ATTACK. THE INTRUDER ACTED SO QUICKLY.
BUT YES, WE FOUND KARTÉ. SHE WAS LOCKED IN A STORAGE CONTAINER, HER ROBES STOLEN, BUT SHE IS UNHARMED.
GOOD.

WOULD YOU CARE TO JOIN US FOR SUPPER? THE OTHERS AS WELL.
NO, THANK YOU. WE WISH TO ACCOMPANY CAPTAIN TYPHO FOR ANOTHER SECURITY CHECK.
WE FAILED YOU.
YOU *DIDN'T.* EVERYTHING'S FINE.

A FEAST FIT FOR A DELEGATION.

THANK YOU. YOU SAVED MY LIFE.
YOU SAID I REMIND YOU OF ANAKIN. YOU REMIND ME OF HIM. YOU BOTH HAVE THE SAME UNFLINCHING DESIRE TO HELP OTHERS.

IS THAT ENOUGH, THOUGH? I WANT TO HELP, BUT...
...AM I GOOD ENOUGH?

OF COURSE YOU ARE! AND IT'S YOUR PASSION THAT MAKES YOU A GOOD JEDI.

BUT I GUESS THAT LEADS TO ME BEING IMPULSIVE.

ANAKIN CAN BE IMPULSIVE, TOO. BUT HE USES THAT TO HIS ADVANTAGE. SO DO YOU.
AHSOKA, YOU TAKE A STANCE. YOU KNOW WHAT TO FIGHT FOR, AND YOU NEVER GIVE UP. THAT'S IMPORTANT.

TO PEACE!
AND FRIENDSHIP.
THE END.

Star Wars: Forces of Destiny "Ahsoka & Padmé"
Variant cover B artwork by Elsa Charretier

STAR WARS FORCES OF DESTINY™

COLLECT THEM ALL!

Set of 5 Hardcover Books ISBN: 978-1-5321-4291-8

Hardcover Book ISBN
978-1-5321-4292-5

Hardcover Book ISBN
978-1-5321-4293-2

Hardcover Book ISBN
978-1-5321-4294-9

Hardcover Book ISBN
978-1-5321-4295-6

Hardcover Book ISBN
978-1-5321-4296-3